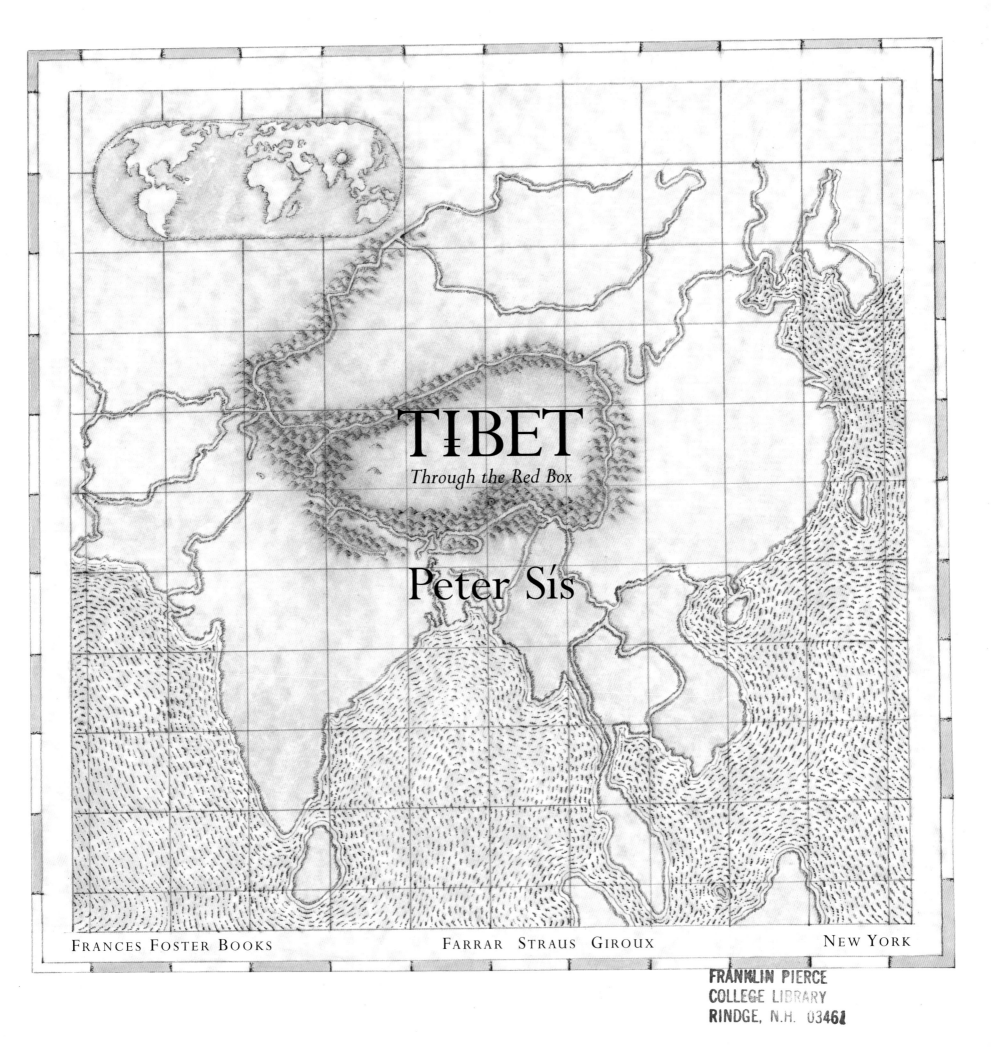

TIBET
Through the Red Box

Peter Sís

FRANCES FOSTER BOOKS   FARRAR STRAUS GIROUX   NEW YORK

From son to father and father to son

Copyright © 1998 by Peter Sís
All rights reserved
Distributed in Canada by Douglas & McIntyre Ltd.
Color separations by Hong Kong Scanner Craft
Printed in the United States of America by Berryville Graphics
Designed by Lilian Rosenstreich
First edition, 1998

Library of Congress Cataloging-in-Publication Data
Sís, Peter.
    Tibet : through the red box / Peter Sís.
      p. cm.
    "A Frances Foster Book."
    ISBN 0-374-37552-6
    1. Tibet (China)—Description and travel. I. Title
    DS786.S548   1998
     951'.5—DC21   97-50175

Grateful acknowledgment is made for the use of the excerpt
from *The Gift* by Vladimir Nabokov, copyright © 1963, with
permission of Vintage Books, a division of Random House, Inc.

Prague, September 19, 1994
The Red Box is now yours.
Love, Father

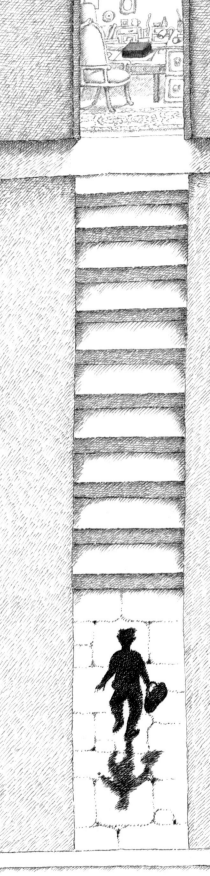

After all these years, my father is calling me home.

I have to hurry.

I am back in Prague, in our old house.

Where is everyone?

I climb the stairs to my father's study.

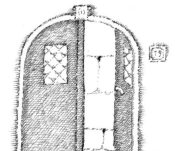

The red box is on the table, waiting.

But I am worried about my father, who is not here.

I unlock the box with a rusty little key.

Inside lies my father's diary—pages and pages of fragile paper covered with faded handwriting and fine drawings and maps blending into the text, all of it barely holding together, like brittle autumn leaves. Butterfly wings and pieces of cloth are pressed between its pages; and in the bottom of the box there are beads, buttons, and fragments of stones. It's like an ancient anthill or a grave of memories buried in the sweet smell of honey, rosin, and sandalwood . . .

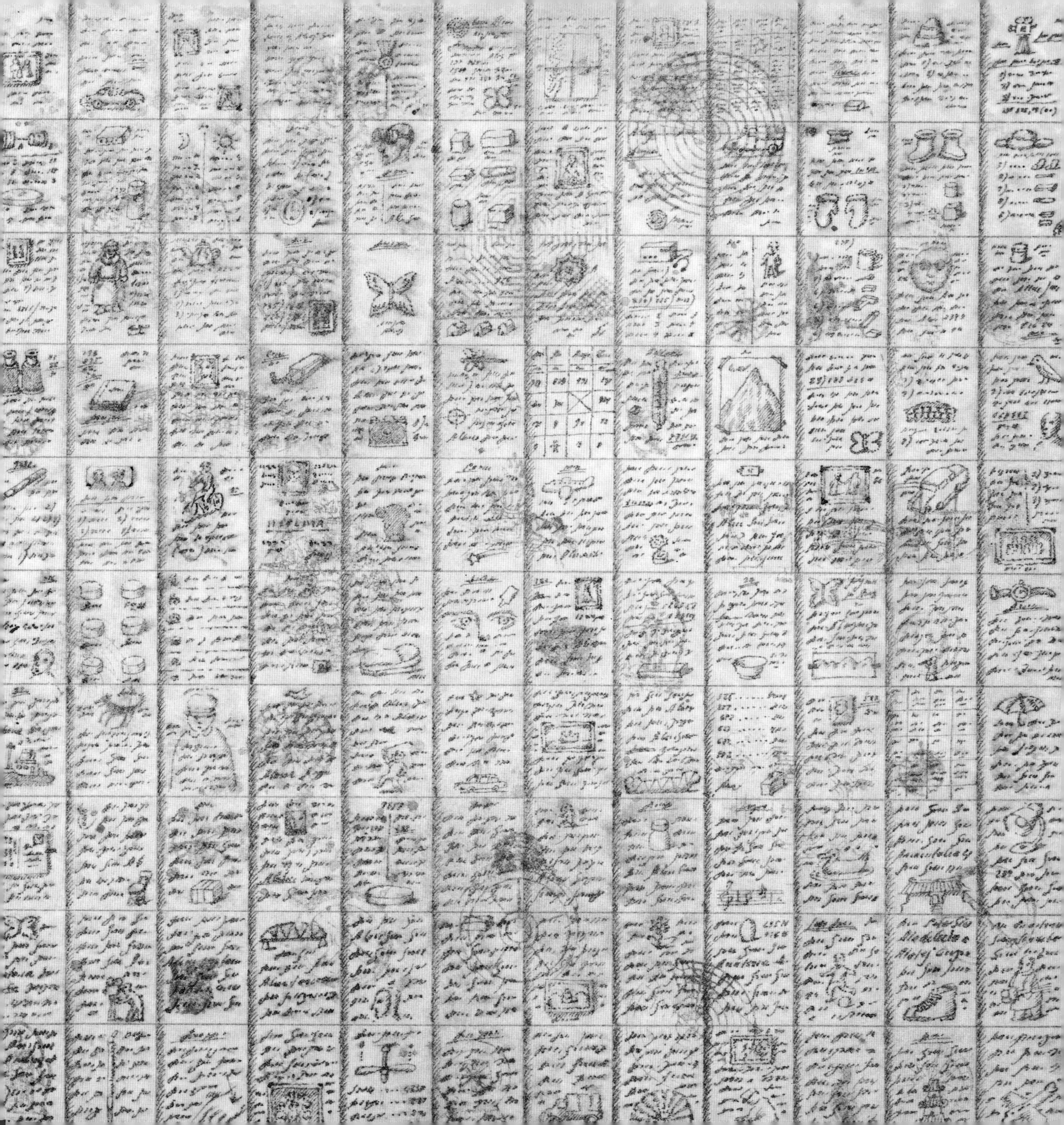

THE STORY OF THE RED BOX

When I was little, my father, who was a filmmaker, spent a lot of time with me. We played for hours in the magic garden of our house, which was en-closed by a high, safe wall. Sometimes my mother let me go with him when he was working on his films. Then one day he left on an expedition that took him far away. He said he would be home for Christmas, and then he was gone. And gone. At first my mother got letters from him, and then they stopped coming. I would sit in his study, gazing at the green wall behind his table, looking at his boxes and his collection of butterflies, trying to imagine his face. Christmases came and went. I could not remember him clearly anymore.

I grew fast, perhaps too fast. There was a problem with my spine, and the doctor prescribed special exercise classes. Then one day I jumped from the high wall of our garden, and suddenly I could not move at all. I was in a white bed in a white room, and I couldn't move my arms or legs. I remember nothing except that another Christmas was coming. Then I remember opening my eyes and someone—a stranger—was sitting by my bed, talking to me in his deep voice. He was holding my hands and telling me a story about a jingle-bell boy. And I could feel my hands! And I knew the stranger. He told me another story about some gentle giants, while touching my feet. And I could feel my feet, and I recognized the man. After he had told me a third story about a magic lake, he kissed me on my cheek. I felt the kiss and could see colors again.

The man was my father. He had been gone for a long time, and now he had come home—for Christmas.

After my father returned, I could walk again.

My father wanted to talk to his friends about all that he had seen and been through, but none of them knew what the world was really like outside their own country, and they probably wouldn't have believed him anyway. So he told me, over and over again, his magical stories of Tibet, for that is where he had been. And I believed everything he said. I would try to draw the things he talked about, things I could hardly imagine. But then I drew less and less. With school, piano, English and French lessons, there was no time. And as I got older I became bored with his stories and eventually stopped listening.

I was an adult before I started thinking about them again, and gradually I began to understand the significance and magnitude of the expedition my father had been sent on when I was a child. I could appreciate the garden of my childhood.

I was born a few years after the Second World War and just a year after the Communist takeover of my country, Czechoslovakia. The Soviet Union was our big brother and leader. Red flags and stars were everywhere; we were surrounded by an iron curtain. Because of my father's growing reputation as a documentary filmmaker, he was drafted into the army film unit and ordered to go to China to make films and teach filmmaking. It was supposed to be only a two-month assignment.

He had hoped to be able to pursue his passion, filming butterflies and rare plants; instead, he was teaching the Chinese how to make documentary films. They wanted to document the building of a highway in the Himalaya. Construction had already begun. So my father found himself in the highest mountain range in the world, in what was described to him as a remote western province of China. Gradually, he learned that this "western province" was actually Tibet and that he had been sent to film a military operation—the construction of a highway that would open Tibet to China. An act of nature separated him from the project and he was subsequently lost in Tibet, where he lived through unimaginable experiences and met with the Boy-God-King in the forbidden city of Lhasa. Six months later, the Chinese army arrived with the Lhasa highway. My father witnessed its arrival and saw Tibet undergo great changes. He was lucky to get home at all.

While my father was in China and Tibet, he kept a diary, which was later locked in a red box. We weren't allowed to touch the box. The stories I heard as a little boy faded to a hazy dream. It was not until I myself had gone far, far away and received the message from my father that I became interested in the red box again.

I begin to read my father's diary.

THE BEGINNING

I am leaving in the dark. The children are unaware and sleeping, safely tucked in their beds. A last farewell kiss, and I am gone.

By plane to Moscow and an endless wait for the plane to Beijing . . . Then the official welcome, speeches, exchange of gifts. We're taken through the dusty, crowded streets to our hotel. Everything is different—smells, horizons, beds, bathrooms. The food is delicious yet different, too—chicken with peanuts, sweet and sour dishes, always rice and tea. We struggle with chopsticks. Pepi, my cameraman, and I are wondering what lies ahead for us. Let's hope the world of cameras and developing 35 mm film is universal.

We meet with the film committee. Everything is fine, but they suggest we take our class to a real location. What might that be? Coincidentally, there is a big construction project going on in some mountain area, a mountain road. In fact, it's the highest highway in the world. It would give ample opportunity to all the apprentice cameramen to shoot work in action—drilling, blasting, digging, loading. It sounds made to order.

We are introduced to our students. They all seem to be in uniform, but then everybody here is. We're supposed to start our class tomorrow, but it's hard to communicate. I don't speak Chinese, and even though they tell me they speak Russian, they don't understand me when I do. Perhaps it won't matter. They'll just watch us decide how and what to shoot.

We're flown by rickety army transport plane to the mountains.

The mountains are the Himalaya! It's an amazing, overpowering, larger-than-life range of solid peaks. How would anyone attempt to build a gate here, not to

mention a road? We are observing an unbelievable military-like operation with thousands of workers dangling by ropes, digging into the rocky mountainsides. Others are blasting holes, bulldozing and excavating the earth. It's mostly human labor, without machinery. How shall we get this on film? Shoot from above? From below? What about the dust? The early sunset? The sun disappears in midafternoon, and then the fog descends. The technical problems are enormous; just keeping the film warm is a challenge. Our equipment weighs hundreds of pounds. We're not sure of our students' abilities and won't know what we've got until the film comes back from the labs in Beijing.

On top of all this, we are told not to venture away from the building site. The road will lead to a remote part of China that is populated by primitive people who are ruled by "Black Monks." The region is called "The Dark Mountain" . . . The highway will bring medical supplies, information, and civilization, and open this world to the twentieth century.

It's going to take more than two months. I'm sure Alenka and the children will be understanding. I have already seen a bird that resembles a boubou, with its long neck and yellow feathers. In the mountains I may see plants and butterflies I haven't even dreamed about.

We keep hearing about bands of brigands in these mountains.

Day after day, we watch the thousands of workers, suspended by ropes, digging into the walls of the Himalaya. The road looks like a cut into a beautiful cake.

So far, no letters from home.

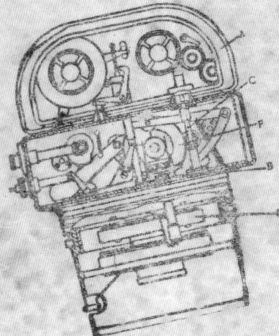

We're filming the steep western side of the mountain when the wall suddenly collapses, carrying workers, machinery, and all with it. Pandemonium! When the dust settles, we—my cameraman, Pepi, and two of our students—realize we cannot get back and have no choice but to try to go on and rejoin the construction crew later. We hope! We have some provisions, a tent, water pouches, and other supplies, but how long can we survive with only this?

Our film equipment is too heavy to carry. We have to leave part of it behind.

We've got to keep climbing . . .

I wish we had a map . . .

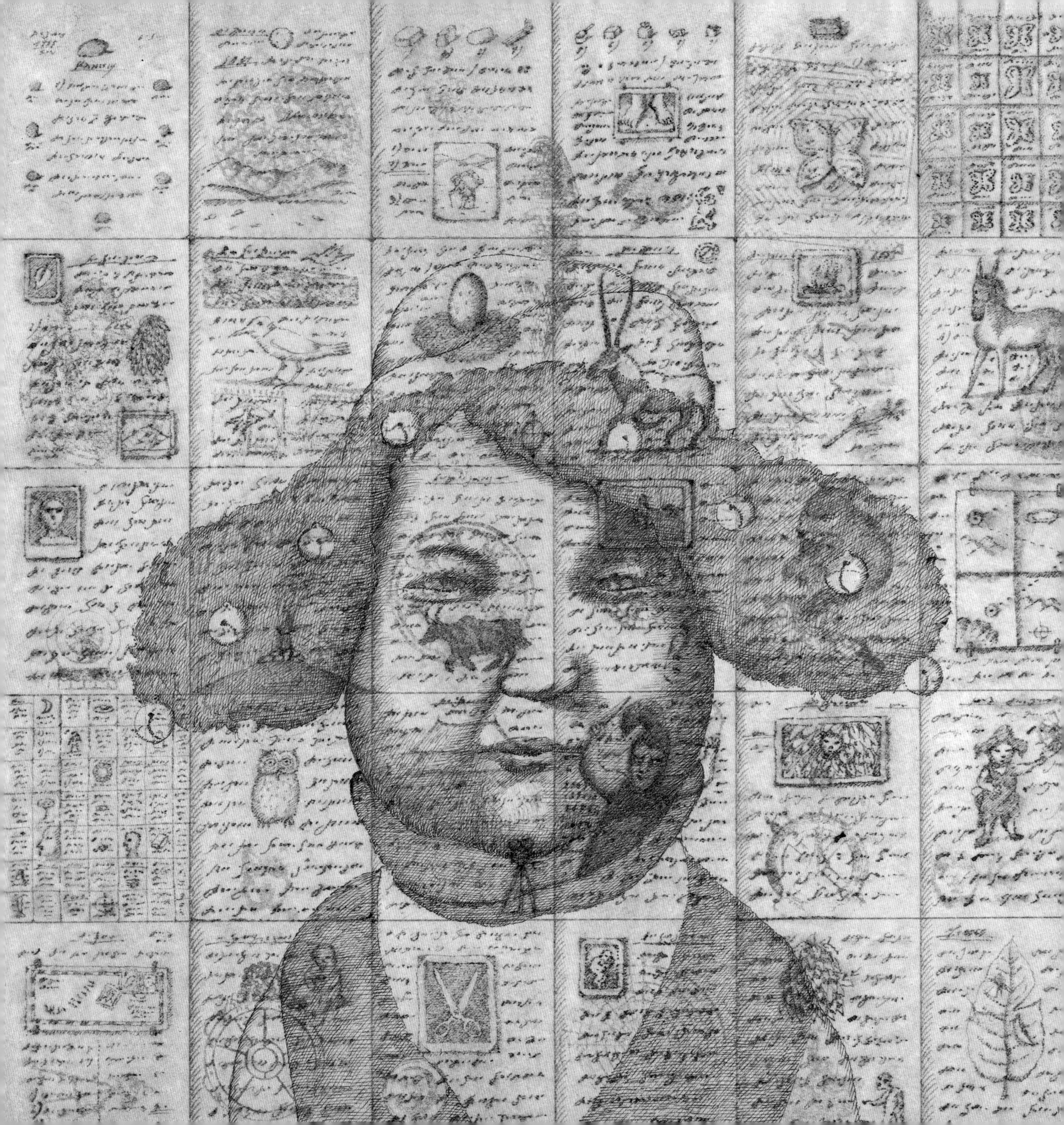

It's the fourth day of our ordeal . . . A chilly misty morning. We've been traveling into the unknown for days . . . The nights are miserable. We lie close together, unable to sleep—it's too cold! We are trying to find water in a giant rhododendron forest when we hear the unexpected sound of bells. A Christmas sort of sound, like jingle bells.

Out of the vegetation emerges a boy dressed in red rags. Little bells are fastened to his clothes. To my absolute astonishment, he opens his pouch and hands over a letter! It's a letter from my family . . .

THE JINGLE-BELL BOY

I first heard the tale of the jingle-bell boy when I was lying in the white bed in the white room.

Later I would try to draw what my father was talking about. But what did I know then? Maybe I should try again . . .

But what do I know now?

My father was lost in a mountain forest of giant rhododendrons. He and his companions didn't know which way to go. All of a sudden, he heard the gentle tinkling of bells. Out of the foliage appeared a little boy dressed all in red. He had jingling bells on his hat, around his wrists, and attached to his pouch and his spear. He was smiling, and he gave my father a letter addressed to him—a letter from Prague. My father was amazed; how could this be? He had been waiting for a letter from his family for a long time, but to have it reach him in the middle of nowhere? That was unbelievable! How had the boy found him? Was my father not as lost as he thought he was?

My father wanted to give the jingle-bell boy a present

and remembered a pair of scissors he had brought to cut film and labels. The boy seemed pleased and fascinated by this strange tool, which he opened and closed and tried out on tufts of grass and on leaves. They offered the boy a place by the fire for the night. My father was hoping to learn where they were and how to find their way out; he tried drawing maps in the dirt, but he couldn't make himself understood.

When Father awoke the next morning, the boy was gone. Then Father noticed a rhododendron leaf with an unusual cut, and then another and another. He knew as he followed the scissor cuts they would lead him out of the forest and through the mountainous maze of valleys and ridges.

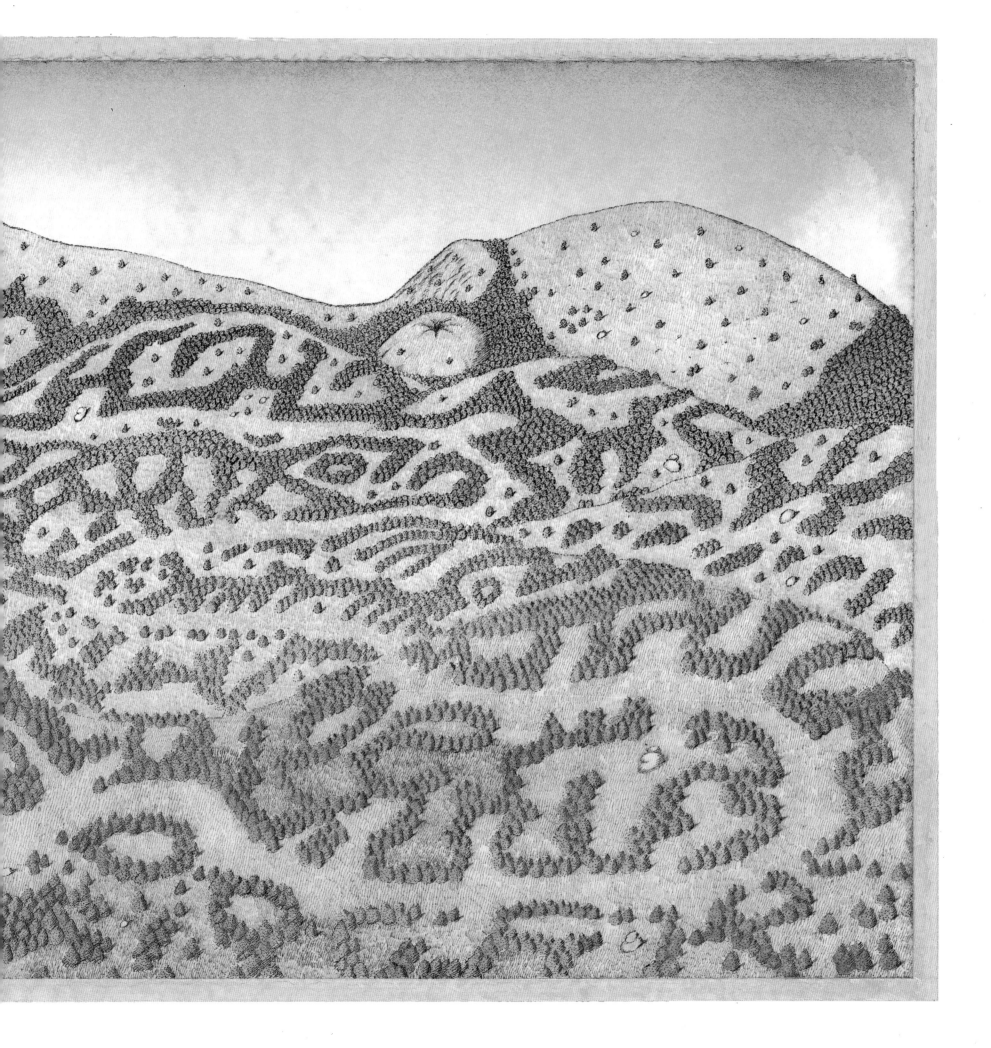

RED IS THE COLOR OF FIRE. RED WAS THE SUNSET IN THE VALLEY AS WELL AS THE EVENING LIGHT

IN MY FATHER'S ROOM. HOW MANY TIMES, THROUGHOUT MY LIFE, HAD I SAT IN THIS ROOM

As I am reading the diary,

the room becomes red.

The letter is covered with stamps and postmarks and was sent many months ago. I give the "mailman" a pair of scissors—one of the few things I can get along without. Next morning he's gone, but under a stone by the campfire there is an ancient map on bark paper. It says to me, "Welcome to the land of magic."

According to the map the boy left, we are in Thibett. If this is Tibet, it is amazing. I vaguely remember stories in the illustrated magazines about a forbidden country and its castle-like monasteries hidden in the mountains. As far as I know, no Czech has ever been here.

Everywhere you look, you see mountains. They're like the organ pipes in the churches of Europe—endless organ pipes.

We meet our first "Dark Mountain" natives—nomads who stick out their tongues at us. (We later learn it is to prove there are no lies on them.) Everybody carries a prayer wheel. They call it ch'a-kor. They haven't seen foreigners before, but still they invite us into their tents to get warm and they give us

tsampa—made with roasted barley flour—and strong tea with butter made from the milk of domestic yaks. We have also seen enormous herds of wild yaks.

Yaks are the most important animals here. They provide milk, meat, and transport, and their long underfur is woven into clothes. The coarse outer hair is used for tents. We follow our map and a big caravan of yaks carrying wool and tea across the plateau. We feast on wild onions and strawberries.

There was no regular mail distribution in the Himalaya, since Tibet was not in the world postal-union territory. Postal runners ran in long-distance relays carrying the mail in waterproof canvas pouches. The mail runners dressed in red as a sign of their importance and wore bells on their clothing to announce their approach. They carried spears to defend themselves against wild animals.

(One and a half months have passed, during which my father has filled twenty pages of the diary.)

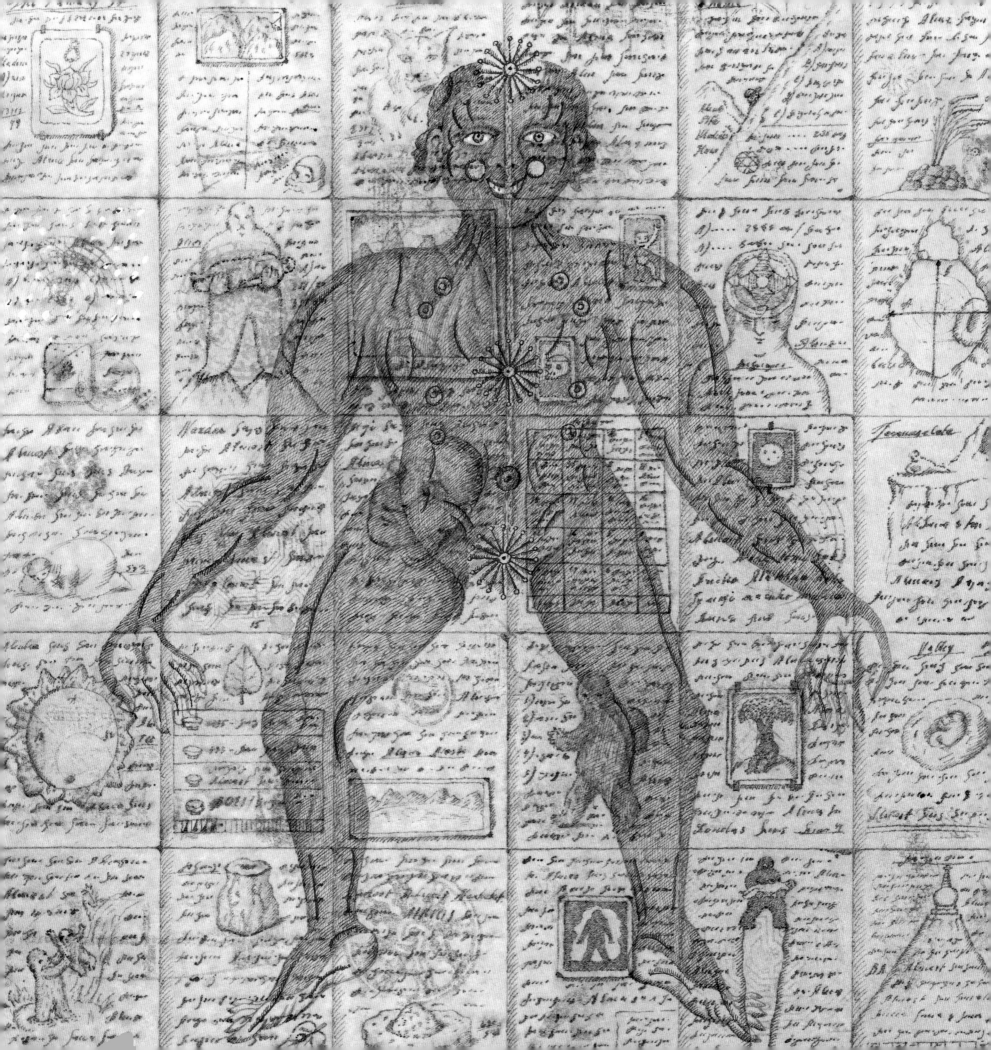

If we really are in the Dark Mountain, it is not only beautiful but peaceful. We've met no brigands yet and the colorful people neither look nor act like the primitive inhabitants of a dark empire we were cautioned against. They seem to have no knowledge of the coming highway . . .

Buddhist monasteries rise up out of the mountains. The monks are very kind and helpful, and they have shown us some rare treasures. In one monastery we're shown a mural with a white-and-red palace they call the Potala, where the living Buddha resides. They say it is in Lhasa. We're also shown an incredible skull decorated with precious stones, looking human but much bigger and more powerful. We are told it is the skull of a Yeti, a giant snowman.

We are slowly learning the language. <u>Yeh ten</u> is a wild mountain creature. <u>Metoh Kangami</u> is Abominable Snowman. <u>Tambo</u> is 1, <u>Niba</u> is 2, <u>Sumbo</u> 3. <u>Cama</u> means cow and <u>Ta</u> horse.

The Chinese call this country <u>fan,</u> the common term for barbarians. Moslem writers in the ninth century called it Tubbet and Tibbat. From them, it came to us through Marco Polo as Tibet.

A monk shows us an old illustrated manuscript of a Yeti creation tale. He tells us the story over a bowl of tea.

YETI CREATION TALE

The patron of Tibet, Chenrezi, sent his disciple, a holy monkey, to be a hermit in the mountains . . . The monkey heard an ogress crying and took pity on her and married her. They had six children and they multiplied and became big hairy people . . . the Yetis! When the first kings descended from the sky, they eventually became the Tibetan people.

THE VALLEY OF THE GIANTS

The story of the Yetis is another one that I first heard when I was confined to the white bed. I used to draw them, but their magic was beyond my comprehension . . . They were one-eyed giants, bigger than our house.

My father was crossing a mountain pass when a sudden snowstorm caught him by surprise. He became separated from his companions and was looking for shelter, but the winds and snow pushed him to the ground. He probably lost consciousness but has some vague memory, like a dream, of being lifted and carried. He awoke in a dark cave, on a bed of leaves and branches. Next to his bed was a small stone container with a potion tasting like honey and herbs. He tried to get up, but he was too weak and just slept and slept. Each time he awakened, he found more potion and drank it. It must have been nutritious, for soon his strength began to return. All the time, he had a feeling that he was being watched over.

One day he was strong enough to crawl out of the cave onto a rocky ledge overlooking a green valley squeezed between the mountain peaks. It looked like a painting of the Garden of Eden. After his eyes had adjusted to the light, he noticed giant fairy beings moving gently in a kind of slow motion throughout the valley. Some appeared to be working, gathering, tending to young ones; others seemed to be playing in the streams and waterfalls. He could also see more caves and burrows. Was it a lost civilization? He did not know. He was tired and crawled back into the cave. But now he was trying not to sleep. His eyes were half closed when he saw a giant being, eight to nine feet tall, put food next to his bed.

He couldn't tell how many days and nights, perhaps weeks, he stayed, recovering his strength and observing the life of the gentle giants in the valley from his precipice perch. Then the time came when he was ready to try to go, and he made the steep descent from the ledge to the valley. Traveling toward the dawn, he left the valley only to come to an abyss so wide that no man could ever cross it. Out of the shadows his giant Yeti friend emerged, lifted him in his arms, and with one leap carried my father across the abyss. As my father made his way down the mountain, he tried to convince himself that the land of the gentle giants was just a dream caused by the very thin mountain air. And then he rejoined the rest of his group, which had almost given up on ever seeing him again.

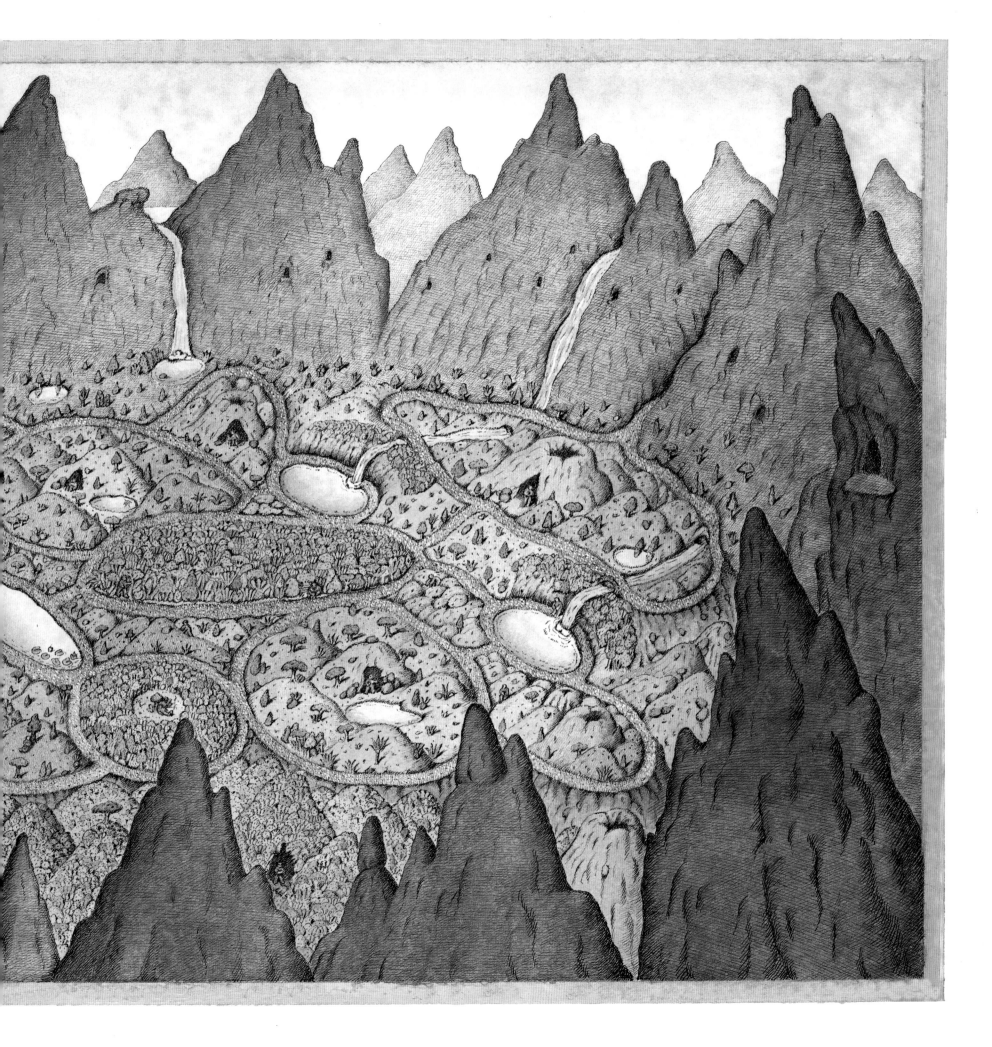

GREEN REPRESENTS THE EARTH. THE WALLS OF MY FATHER'S ROOM WERE GREEN,

THE PEACEFUL GREEN OF MEADOWS AND TREES.

I continue reading,

BUT THE PLANTS MY FATHER FILMED WERE ALSO GREEN.

and the room slowly turns green.

. . . Sick for a few weeks after getting lost in a snowstorm . . . Strange dreams . . . Hallucinations . . . My friends left me for a while in the care of a farmer.

We are continuing into the mountains on the way to Lhasa . . .

The people we meet are gentle and helpful . . . Great sense of humor. The local costume is beautiful. We watch a shooting competition with bows and arrows. The special arrowheads make a whistling noise. This is one of the sports of the villagers. Horse races, too. Competition is fierce but friendly.

The typical farmer's home has a flat roof with brightly colored prayer flags at the corners. Lots of thornwood and dried dung are stacked on the roof for cooking. We drink tea, tea, and more tea. I learn that the best tea water comes from a glacier and runs through leaves of plants and through the ground into a waiting container. After three years, this water is poured into a porcelain container with a few leaves of tea. When the leaves open, the tea is ready to drink. A whole house can share the fragrance of one bowl.

We have yet to encounter tyrannical monks or brigands.

We wonder when we will meet up with the construction units. Surely somewhere before Lhasa, for that is where we are heading.

What is my family thinking or doing? When will I hear from them?

Everywhere we see stupas (<u>chorten</u>, in the Tibetan language)—round domes on a square base with a spike emerging upward: the base representing green earth, the dome signifying blue water, the spike standing for red fire and topped by a half-moon, for air, and a sun representing infinite space. Stupas are Buddhist monuments—some are large and grand, others are very crude and simply made. Sometimes stones are piled up to represent stupas. We see worshippers circling these sacred objects in a clockwise direction, with the stupa always on their right. Lamas, sages, and saints are buried in the stupas.

November 24. All my thoughts go back to you, Alenka. It is so wonderful that you came into this spinning world twenty-nine years ago today. I wanted to surprise you with a huge bunch of roses. I swear to God I will come as soon as I can. Until then, I am sending you a kiss, my deposit for the future. Darling, I will celebrate your birthday by trekking toward Lhasa.

December 6. Our wedding anniversary . . . Hana's birthday . . . and in some parts of the world they're celebrating St. Nicholas. We celebrate Christmas with a little tree branch decorated with color-film wrappers . . .

(Diary page numbers jump from 220 to 286, covering four to six months.)

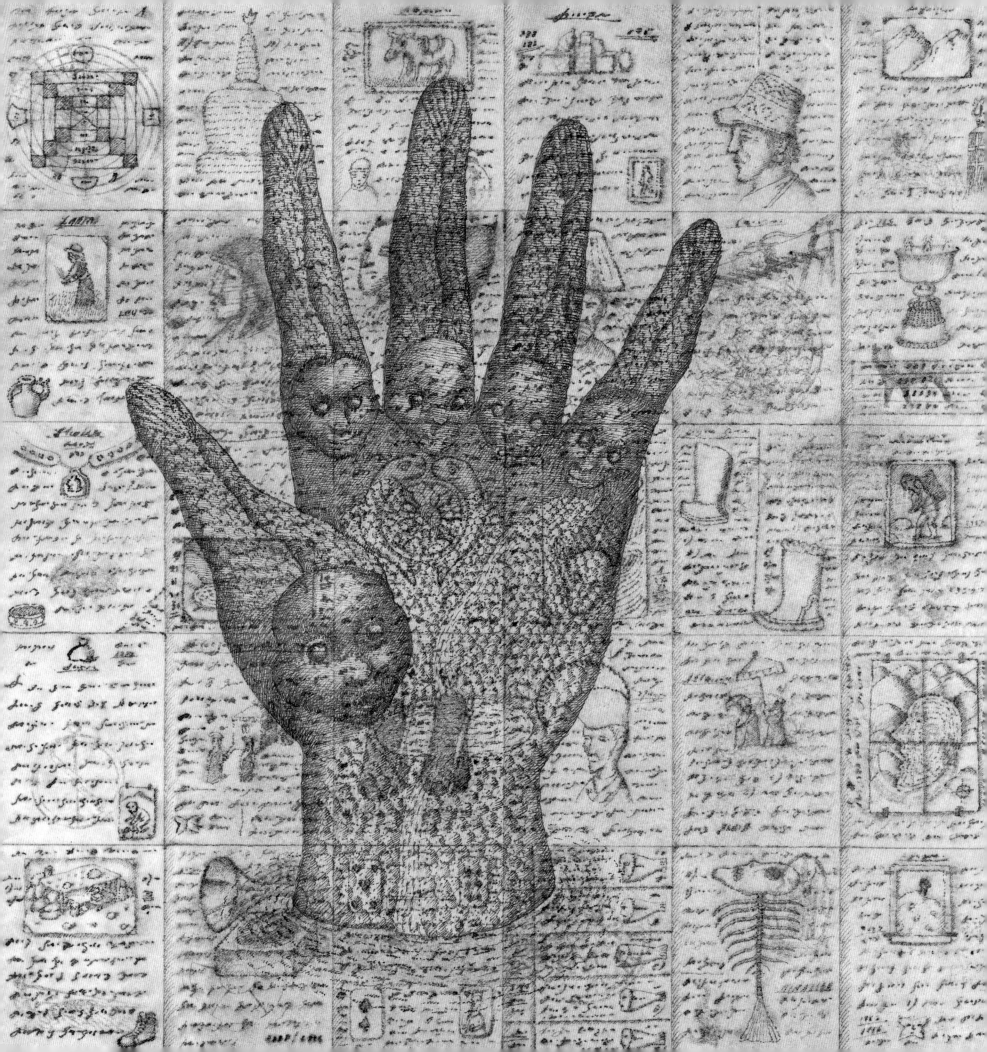

We are high in the mountains again, and I hope we are nearing Lhasa. The air is very thin and the trekking rough. The wind is always blowing. Tibet is the highest country in the world—the roof of the world—with villages as much as 10,000 feet above sea level. Its highest mountains are 25,000 feet and more.

We see symbols of fish (gser-na) in many places and are told they symbolize spiritual freedom because water allows fish to swim freely.

Have come to a clear blue lake in the mountains with a monastery above it. While we are sharing some tea with the monks, they tell us another creation story:

A CREATION TALE

First there was light and water and wind. And from the wind came the egg, which was the world. The very first egg was dark red—like a sunset. Next came an egg that was the color of brass. The third egg was a metallic blue. The fourth egg was golden. A long time after the golden world, our universe was born as a white egg—a very fragile egg floating on the water.

We see lamas flying on giant kites. People tell stories of lamas who have the power to transform themselves into wild creatures or birds. They are also trained in secret regimens of breathing and body control to move with extraordinary speed. We are told they can travel as if carried on wings.

We learn that the lake where we are camping is a sacred place. The whole land of Tibet is considered to be a goddess. The mountains house mythical creatures and various Buddha forms. The lakes are oracle mirrors—they tell you how to advance in life. It is said that in prehistoric times Tibet was one large lake. Bit by bit, it dried up, and the country was covered by a juniper forest with magic turquoise lakes scattered here and there. Our lake is home to some unusual fish—huge, silent carp-like creatures with big eyes, long whiskers, and quiet faces.

Night comes . . . No stars, just darkness. The whispering lake is all we hear. We decide to leave in the morning.

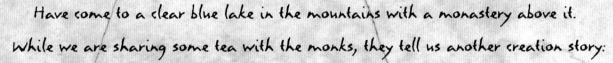

THE BLUEST LAKE

I remember this story from the white bed, too, and I drew many a fish with a human face. I still do. Even humans with fish faces.

I am scared of clear deep lakes because of this story and another story from my childhood

of a German army unit frozen in the clear cold waters of a lake, looking as if they might still be alive.

After weeks of trekking, my father's party reached a beautiful blue lake. It was so clear he could see the surrounding mountain range and the monastery reflected in it. When he dipped his tired, aching feet into the icy water, some huge fish silently appeared from the deep and touched his toes. He returned their stares and realized he was looking into the faces of people. Human faces! He quickly pulled his feet out of the water and went back to the camp, just in time to welcome a litter carrying the High Lama from the nearby monastery. They exchanged greetings and tea, and the Lama told my father the story of the lake. Its name sounded like An'n.

From the beginning of time, the lake had been an oracle and a sacred burial place. Some years before, around the turn of the twentieth century, a caravan arrived with two white traders. Among their wares were large tins of dried milk, which they sold and bartered. When the traders saw the fish with human features in the lake, they realized that this discovery could make them rich. They decided to take some specimens back with them in the now empty milk tins. The lamas tried to tell them this was not a good idea, but the traders wouldn't listen and bribed some local peasants to help them transport the fish to one of the seaports in India. The peasants took the bribe and the fish and pretended to start on their journey, when actually they hid behind the mountain. Then in the dark of night they released the fish back into the lake.

And what happened to the merchants? The High Lama took my father into the little hut. He showed him the dusty cot, the table with an unfinished card game for two, the half-smoked pipe, and a rusty gramophone with a record on it. Then he led my father to the bluest lake, where the fish were swimming close to shore. He pointed out two with distinctly European features.

BLUE IS THE COLOR OF WATER, OCEANS, AND SKY, THE COLOR OF FREEDOM AND FLYING.

IT WAS A RARE COLOR IN THE LANDLOCKED COUNTRY OF MY CHILDHOOD,

It's getting darker,

and the room is bathed in a blue light

I feel we are close to the Potala, even though no one talks about it. We're in the Valley of Hungry Dogs. Our tent is pitched directly on the road, by a white, red, and blue bridge—though it's not really a road, just stones arranged in a loose line.

We see people with tattooed faces. It's very cold.

Small Tibetans with large flails are threshing wheat. The flailing sticks are covered with leather and hinged with a wooden knob. Four men and five women sing as they work—hum-hum Amare a-a-a-ca Pe-ca—in full voices that come from deep in their throats. They seem to be conversing in song. At the end of the line, a little girl tries to keep the rhythm and the pace.

Everybody gives us <u>chadaks</u>, scarves of friendship. The people are really very friendly and smiley. They love to laugh.

They have no desire to be rich. Gold apparently means nothing to them. They carry gold dust in hollow horns to give to the gods. I offer to buy things from them, but they don't want to sell anything. They give them to me.

They're in no hurry to get anywhere fast. What's the use of getting somewhere and then being bored?

But I feel a great need to hurry to the Potala and warn the Dalai Lama about what is coming. The road is truly an amazing undertaking and engineering feat. It might well bring hospitals, electricity, and technology, but little roads will then go to the lake, to the Valley of the Yetis, to the caves and monasteries. What will it take away? It might take more than it brings. I have to explain all this and make the Boy-God-King understand what it means. I have to make my students understand.

Tibet is ruled by the Dalai Lama. There have been fourteen, in succession, each one a reincarnation of his predecessor. Dalai means ocean in Mongol, ocean of wisdom. When a Dalai Lama dies, the search for his reincarnation begins at once, aided by the oracles, portents, and dreams, until a little boy possessing the unique qualities is found. In addition to showing special physical traits, he must pass other tests and be able to identify the late Dalai Lama's belongings among a pile of objects.

Potala is home to the living Dalai Lama and to his sumptuous golden tomb when he dies. Built on a red hill, the awesome structure, with more than a thousand rooms, can be seen for miles. The round outside towers were fortifications, but legend says they are wings to lift Potala to safety if it is threatened.

We see wheels of life painted everywhere, symbolizing life as it really is. In the center is a rooster, standing for passion; a snake, for hatred; and a boar, signifying delusion.

A village of stupas—red, white, and black—with camels wandering around them.

There are huge paintings of Buddhas on mountainsides.

How long has it been since I have seen a landscape without mountains?

I have convinced my companions to hurry. We get up while it's still dark. I am reminded of long-ago winters when my grandmother used to wake me for school. Our breath is steam in the frigid air. We walk all day. I think I can hear the roar of the first trucks arriving on the new road. I must find the young Boy-God-King, the fourteenth Dalai Lama, while there's still time.

The sun is setting; it is 3 p.m. In the misty valley ahead of us, we see the first buildings of the forbidden city, Lhasa. The setting sun is reflected in the hundreds of little marsh lakes. In the distance we can see Potala. We stand speechless, enjoying that view. We come to a river. The boat that carries us across is made from yak hides. In the red sun of the dying day, we feel somehow special.

(Following this entry, one half page was deleted from the diary in 1956.)

Peter, we are using the same kind of boats as the old Babylonians!

POTALA

The story of Potala, as I remember it from the white bed, is hazy. The jingle-bell boy with his little spear gets confused in my mind with the Boy-God-King, the fourteenth Dalai Lama, sitting under the peacock umbrella on a golden throne.

My father reached Potala to find it surrounded by a sea of military tents. He had no idea how to get in. Then he noticed a cut here, a cut there, in a shrub, the grass, a leaf, a tent. The cuts showed him a path through the camp, to a gate, up some stairs to another gate, down a corridor, and into a room. But Potala is a magic palace with a thousand rooms—a room for every emotion and heart's desire. There is a room covered with stars, portending the future, and a room with the coffins of the eight-foot-tall golden people of ancient times. There are rooms showing underground rivers, and mountains touching blue skies. There are rooms of hope and rooms of sorrow. Potala embodied wisdom and reason; it dominated the valley, the country, the history of Tibet.

My father walked through its magic rooms, one after the other, until he came to a room with thirteen stupas, the burial places for the thirteen Dalai Lamas, and he realized there was no place left for a fourteenth stupa. What did this mean?

My father had hurried to Potala to tell the Boy-God-King what he thought he understood—about the road coming to Tibet and the outside world pouring in and invading this untouched place at the top of the world. He wanted to mention the magic he had encountered: the jingle-bell boy, the Yetis, and the lake which would be threatened. But as he rushed through the palace (and I know this only from his hints), he realized that beneath the color and splendor of its rooms, and pictured in minute detail and in different aspects, angles, and perspectives, his state of mind was somehow being reflected. It was all here, recorded on these walls, the past and the present. In that short moment, I think my father became who he is today, and in seeing this now, I can understand why he could never clearly write or tell about what he went through in Tibet.

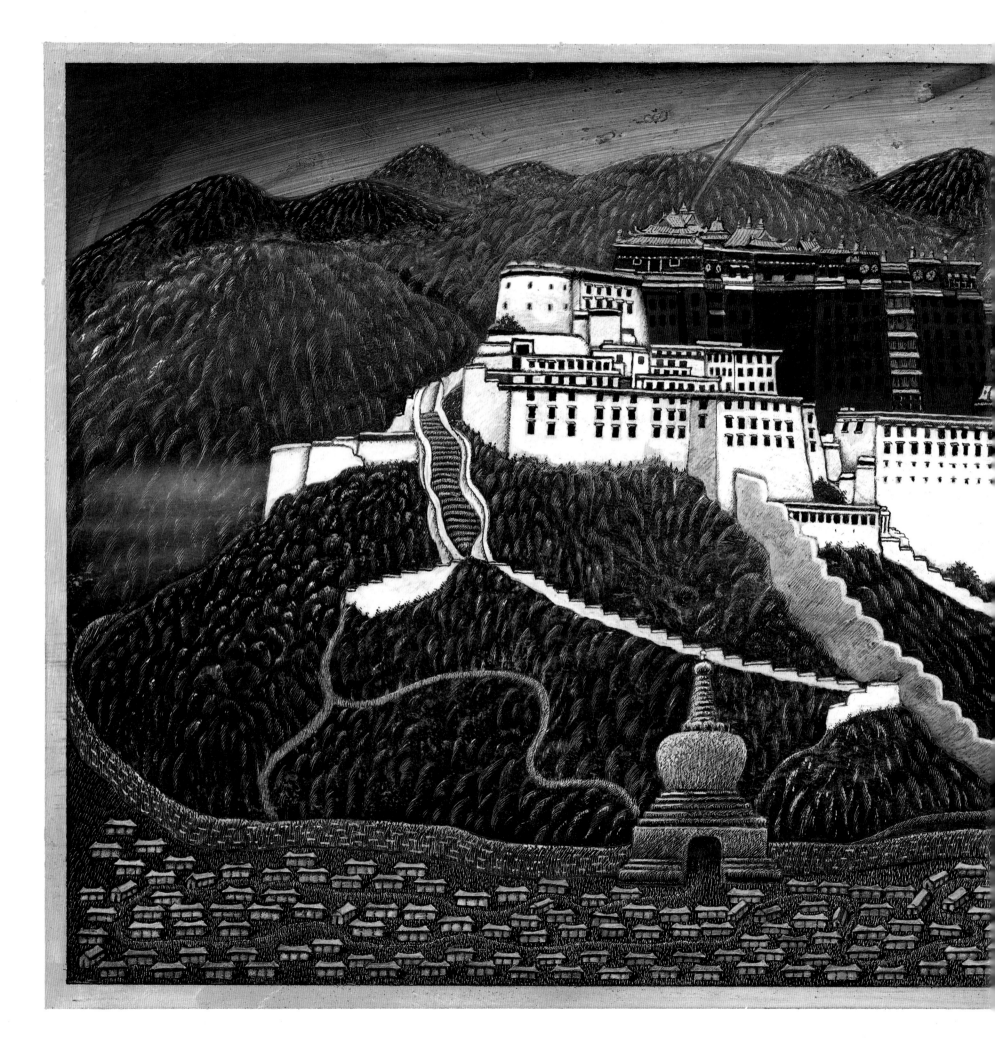

He stumbled into a red room—sunrise and sunset, heart of time.

Next he came to a green room, square and circular, ear of the earth.

After that he entered a blue room, frozen in light and dark, eye of the soul.

And at last a deep, dark room. The Dalai Lama smiled and lifted his hand, and my father heard the gentle jingle of bells.

BLACK IS THE COLOR OF NIGHT, OF MAGIC AND SHADOWS, OF THE UNKNOWN.

YOU CAN PROJECT ALL YOUR DREAMS—OR NIGHTMARES—ONTO BLACK.

I hear the deep voice of my father.

"Why do you sit here in the dark?" he asks.

We close the red box and walk through the streets of the city where I grew up, happy to be together again. My father answers my questions as best he can.

The sky is full of stars.

Now I know that, for me, the red box was Tibet. It is a Tibet I have never been to, and it may be a Tibet that never really existed—a faraway place I first knew as a young child when my father was lost there. Did he get lost for fourteen months or was it longer? Time is measured quite differently by the very young. I wanted him back, and after a long time he did come home, and he told me stories that have made me look for "Tibet" all my life. Only now, after I have visited it through the pages of my father's diary, do I realize that I should not have wanted him back. Or did he ever completely return? Is he still happy and young somewhere in Tibet?

In this desert are preserved traces of an ancient road along which Marco Polo passed six centuries before I did: its markers are piles of stones. Just as I had heard in a Tibetan gorge the interesting drum-like roar which had frightened our first pilgrims, so in the desert during the sandstorms I also saw and heard the same as Marco Polo: "The whisper of spirits calling you aside" and the queer flicker of the air, an endless progression of whirlwinds, caravans and armies of phantoms coming to meet you, thousands of spectral faces in their incorporeal way pressing upon you, through you, and suddenly dispersing . . . When the great explorer was dying, his friends gathered by his bedside and implored him to reject what in his book had seemed incredible to them—to water down its miracles by means of judicious deletions; but he responded that he had not recounted even a half of what he had in fact seen.

—from Vladimir Nabokov's The Gift

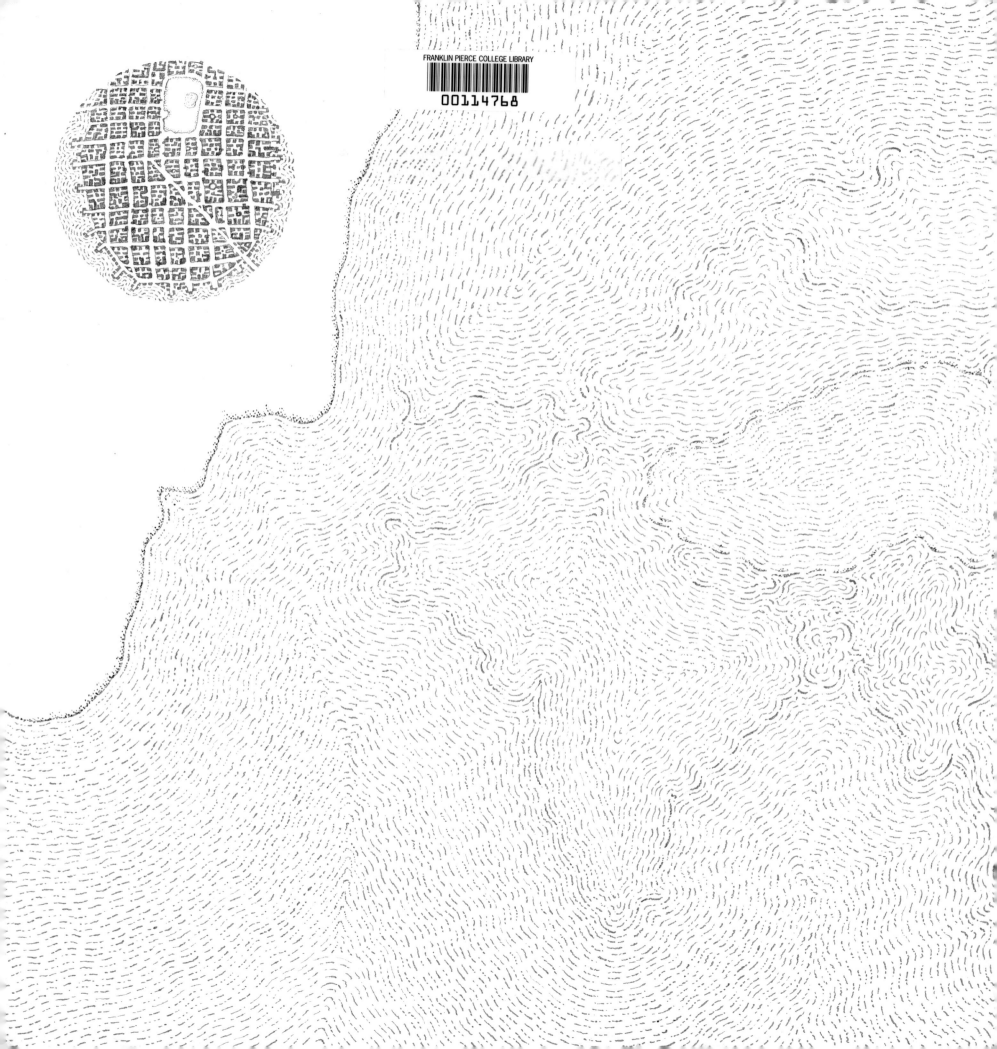